NEVER ON
SHABBAS!

NEVER ON SHABBAS!

by HENRY LEONARD

AUTHOR OF *OPEN YOUR MOUTH AND SAY "OY"*

Favorites from ''DAYENU,'' America's most popular Jewish Cartoon appearing in over 50 Anglo-Jewish Publications.

WITH A FOREWORD BY *HARRY GOLDEN*

ABOUT COMICS, CAMARILLO, CALIFORNIA

FOREWORD

"Dayenu" ("It would have been sufficient for us") is the refrain of a song in the Passover service. The song enumerates the abundant favors which God conferred on Israel and concludes each blessing with the word, "Dayenu," implying that each favor was sufficient to obligate Israel to great thankfulness.

"Dayenu" is a serious term yet it lends itself very well to this particular aspect of our people—the ability to poke fun at ourselves. Even historian Renan, who was not particularly friendly to us, understood this very well; "If you write about Jews you will learn all about humor."

We are a people for whom everything is sacrosanct yet for whom nothing is sacred. Certainly nothing about American-Jewish life is sacred—for which we can only say, Dayenu. To take ourselves too seriously is to make life not only parochial but impossible.

And it is no coincidence that many of the great humorists of the Western world, both in literature and on the stage, have been Jews. The scholar Israel Knox gives us an important insight into this phenomenon, ("Jewish Heritage," February, 1962):

"One of the dominant elements (Jewish humor) was skepticism—the habit of doubt, the shrug of the shoulder . . . What better precaution (than humor) could there be in an environment without guarantees for (Jewish) stability . . ."

Jews understood, too, that nothing makes quicker communication between people than a good laugh. We have to laugh at ourselves because we own both a public and a private *self,* and only by laughing do both *selves* see and understand each other.

Never on Shabbas is a pretty concise analysis of our private *selves,* for which we ought to thank Rabbi Henry Rabin and Leonard Pritikin. If they had given us only the cartoon on page 1, we should have to say, "Dayenu."

Harry Golden

Charlotte, North Carolina
March 1, 1962

This, the second collection of Dayenu (Da-yay-noo) cartoons, follows the outstanding success of OPEN YOUR MOUTH AND SAY "OY." The cartoons are created by Henry Leonard, a name which represents a team. Henry Rabin, Director of the B'nai B'rith Hillel Foundations at Los Angeles City and State Colleges, originates the ideas; the man who actually draws the cartoons is Leonard Pritikin, professionally an advertising director.

Even though the humor, insight and irony are directed at situations in Jewish life, the appeal of Dayenu cartoons is so universal that they delight Jew and non-Jew alike. For readers unfamiliar with Jewish words and terms, we have included a glossary on the next page. As in the previous collection, the cartoons were selected from the series appearing in English-language Jewish publications in many countries throughout the world, to whom we gratefully acknowledge our thanks:

Atlanta, Ga........*The Southern Israelite*
Atlantic City, N. J....*The Jewish Record*
Baltimore, Md.................*The Baltimore Jewish Times*
Birmingham, Ala....*The Jewish Monitor*
Boston, Mass. ....*The Jewish Advocate*
Buffalo, N. Y. ....*The Buffalo Jewish Review*
Camden, N. J. ....*The Voice*
Cape Town, So. Africa....... *The South African Jewish Chronicle*
Chicago, Ill. ....*The Sentinel*
Cincinnati, Ohio...............*Every Friday*
Cleveland, Ohio.......*The Jewish Review and Observer*
Columbus, Ohio.................. *The Ohio Jewish Chronicle*
Denver, Colo..........*The Intermountain Jewish News*
Des Moines, Iowa.......*The News Letter*
Detroit, Mich.....................*The Detroit Jewish News*
Douglaston, N. Y.................*The Scroll*
El Paso, Texas........ *Jewish Community Voice*
Fresno, Cal...................... *Central Valley Jewish Heritage*

Galveston, Texas ....*The Bulletin*
Glasgow, Scotland.....*The Jewish Echo*
Indianapolis, Ind.................*The Indiana Jewish Chronicle*
Jacksonville, Fla............ *The Southern Jewish Weekly*
Jersey City, N. J....*The Jewish Standard*
Johannesburg, South Africa *The Zionist Record*
Long Island, N. Y.......*The Long Island Jewish Press*
Los Angeles, Calif......*The Jewish Voice*
Manchester, England............*The Jewish Telegraph*
Melbourne, Australia.............*Australian Jewish Herald*
Memphis, Tenn.................*The Hebrew Watchman*
Miami, Fla..........*The Jewish Floridian*
Minneapolis, Minn........*The American Jewish World*
Montreal, Canada...........*The Canadian Jewish Chronicle*
Nashville, Tenn.................*The Observer*
Newark, N. J. *American Jewish Ledger*
New York, N. Y.............*The American Examiner*
New York, N. Y.................*World Over*

North Hollywood, Calif. .... *V.J.C.C. Bulletin*	Sydney, Australia .... *The Sydney Jewish News*
Phoenix, Ariz. ..... *Phoenix Jewish News*	Toronto, Canada .... *The Daily Hebrew Journal*
Pittsburgh, Pa. .... *The American Jewish Outlook*	Tucson, Ariz. .... *The Arizona Post*
San Antonio, Tex. .... *The B'nai B'rith Voice*	Vancouver, Canada .... *The Jewish Western Bulletin*
San Diego, Calif. .... *The Southwest Jewish Press*	Washington, D. C. .... *The Jewish Digest*
San Francisco, Calif. .... *The Jewish Community Bulletin*	Washington, D. C. .... *The B'nai B'rith Women's World*
Scranton, Pa. .... *The Argus*	Washington, D. C. .... *The National Jewish Monthly*
South Bend, Ind. .... *Our Community*	Waterbury, Conn. .... *Jewish Community Bulletin*
Springfield, Mass. *Jewish Weekly News*	
St. Paul, Minn. .... *St. Paul Jewish News*	Westchester, N. Y. .... *Westchester Jewish Tribune*
St. Petersburg, Fla. .... *The Suncoast Jewish News*	Winnipeg, Canada .... *The Jewish Post*
Sydney, Australia .... *The Australian Jewish Times*	Worcester, Mass. .... *The Jewish Civic Leader*

GLOSSARY

BAR MITZVAH. Name for confirmed Jewish boy thirteen years old, or name of the ceremony itself.

CHANUKAH. Eight-day festival celebrated in December in honor of ancient Jewish struggle for religious freedom.

CHOMETZ. All leavened food prohibited during Passover.

GALITZEANERS. Jews from Galicia.

GEFILTE FISH. A form of stuffed fish.

GESUNT AUF DEINE KEPPELE. Yiddish expression meaning "May you be blessed."

KIDDUSH. A benediction offered over wine.

LITVAKS. Jews from Lithuania.

MACHER. An important person.

MATZOS. Unleavened bread.

MEZUZAH. A small case, containing Bible passages, found on doorposts of Jewish homes.

NOSHERAI. Sweets or goodies.

NU? Well? So what?

PASSOVER. An eight-day festival commemorating the Jewish deliverance from Egypt.

REBBE. Hebrew teacher or Rabbi.

ROSH HASHANAH. Jewish New Year.

SHABBAS. Sabbath or Saturday.

SHADCHAN. Marriage broker.

SHAMMAS. A Jewish sexton.

SHUL. A synagogue.

SUCCOTH. The Feast of Tabernacles.

SUKKAH. A roofless hut used during the Feast of Tabernacles.

TALLITH. A prayer shawl.

YARMALKE. Skull cap worn in synagogue.

YESHIVAH. An advanced Religious School of Jewish learning.

YOM KIPPUR. The day of atonement.

ZEDE. Grandfather.

"Every Yom Kippur the Rabbi always preaches about our greed and selfishness. Why doesn't he stick to religion?"

"But, Sir, my daughter already donated . . . in Sunday School."

"Next time you'll listen when the Rebbe gives you instructions."

"Rabbi, why does my daddy smoke in the bathroom on Shabbas, and eat there on Yom Kippur?"

Every Jew a Macher

"Ah . . . that's why Mendel is always late on his route. He kisses all the mezuzahs!"

"All right, go and say it . . . it's because we went
fishing on Shabbas."

"As we conclude this Yom Kippur day, I wish to inform our annual guests that our Rosh Hashanah Services will begin next year at 6:45 p.m."

"There goes Beryl, the weightlifter, showing off again!"

"And next on our agenda will be a discussion on an appropriate blessing over Metrecal."

"I don't like to either, David, but we have to for our children's sake."

"Sorry Madam . . . but Chanukah preceded Christmas this year."

"There goes Rabbi Nubkin with his Sukkah-Mobile."

"Rabbi, maybe you can help me. How can I stay away from shul and still not feel guilty about it?"

"And Sam, darling, for Passover, don't forget . . .
bring home a carton of matzos, matzo meal, chopped
nuts, and a big box of bicarb . . ."

"And for the New Year, Mrs. Epstein, there should be peace in the world, prosperity for everybody, freedom for all mankind, and a husband for my daughter, Ellie."

"Take me to your Rabbi."

"Officers of Temple Beth-El, members of the Temple Board, members of my family, mourners and any chance worshippers at this Friday night service . . . "

"Don't you think we should attend at least ONE meeting?"

"It isn't at all like the movie."

"And after the Rabbi's sermon, to help reawaken
the Congregation, we'll sing psalm number . . . "

"On this Bar Mitzvah day I can categorically state I am not a man, but rather a youngster emerging from puberty to advanced adolescence, and sharing with you the ambivalent emotions of which I am bounteously sensitized."

"Look, Noah, you save 'em in your way and I'll save 'em in mine."

"And so, folks, eight nights of Chanukah or not . . .
all I expect is just one present."

"You say you want a Chanukah present? A gesunt
auf deine keppele!"

"Daddy, do Gentiles believe in Christmas, too?"

"And here, Mr. Nathan, is your Rabbi, whom you haven't seen since you joined his temple 15 years ago."

"Rabbi, since I prefer English, please use no Hebrew in the ceremony; since I'm not religious, no theology; and since I'm in a hurry . . . please omit the Sermon."

"But, Rabbi, my head IS covered."

"Lunar Expedition F42 calling Earth . . . Since one day
up here lasts two weeks, Corporal Hyman wants to
know what to do about Shabbas."

"Oh I always bring the baby to shul. The Rabbi's
sermon just works wonders."

"And next week our services will feature a Kiddush
chanted by Cantor Blackstein in three dimensional
stereo."

"Irving, when you leave, must you always kiss me
like I'm a mezzuzah?"

"And don't forget, Mac, . . . for your lunch today in the garment district, it's a kosher corned beef sandwich on rye!"

"David, let's buy this plot . . . it's only five minutes
from the subway."

"The Stork Club or the Copa, Sam. It doesn't matter,
'For whither thou goest, I will go'."

"Nu, Doctor, stop crying already, so I can tell you the rest of my troubles!"

"You can tell it's time for the High Holidays when
Beryl, the shammas, begins oiling the seats."

"And now that our Shabbas services are over, I should like to present and thank the members of our temple choir . . . Mr. Haggarty, Miss Johnson, Mrs. O'Conner and Mrs. Whitney."

"What do I think of my grandchildren? Oh, they're just average."

"Rabbi, this is my husband, David Rabinowitz, and
my two sons, Jerry Robin and Bill Rayburn."

"That's Manny's new all-weather Sukkah. With that weather-eye, the umbrella opens automatically at the first raindrop."

"It says, 'Weight, 150 . . . and take it easy on the
nosherai.' "

"When you're ready, just press this button, then the
ark and pulpit will disappear and you'll have your
full-size basketball court."

"It's the only way Zede will go in."

"Doctor, it must be Yom Kippur time again . . . there are three cantors in the waiting room with laryngitis."

"Girls, now a speech by Rabbi Nubkin, then we'll get
to the more important matters of the afternoon."

"My dear friends, before I speak this evening, I
would like to make a few remarks . . ."

"We interrupt our Shabbas Service to announce that at the end of the fifth inning, the Yankees are leading by . . . "

"Fred, for Passover why don't you get a new Tallith,
and I'LL get a new mink stole?"

"Let's ask the Chief Rabbi where the Mezuzah goes
on this revolving door."

"What did I tell you! In that part of Jersey, Litvaks
DO outnumber Galitzeaners two to one."

"And to think, Son, in my day we just used to call him
'The Shammas'."

"If Churchill and Eisenhower only listened to me years ago, Max, we'd never be in such a mess today."

"Hawkins, please show the Rebbe to Junior's room.
It's time for his Hebrew lesson."

"On our agenda tonight, gentlemen, we have two items: the falling plaster in the men's room, and the future of American Judaism."

"And I wanna give 500 bucks to the Red Cross, and 500 bucks to the Torah V'daas Fund of the 43rd Street Yeshivah."

"Nu, Sarah . . . so a little competition never hurt anyone."

"If you'll just be patient, sir, I'm sure we have a copy
of the Bible somewhere."

"No, it's not a screen test. My cousin Moe is getting married."

"All right, Stern, I'll go to yours tonight, if you go to mine next week."

"Look at him . . . one day in the hospital and he's
already taking his own blood pressure!"

"And I propose, Mr. Chairman, that our answer to this anti-semitic act should be a **COURAGEOUS SILENCE!**"

"We begin our COMPLETE services on page 50. . .
omit the Hebrew on pages 51 to 56 . . . then skip to
the middle of page 64."

"If God helps, and is willing, and we are healthy, and all goes well, and we live . . . I'll see you tomorrow at two o'clock."

"She wants to know what time to light the Shabbas
Candles tonight."

YOU CAN NEVER HAVE ENOUGH DAYENU!

His mother was an Hungarian Jew.
His father, African-American.
Ollie Harrington became the greatest
cartoonist in the Black newspapers of
the twentieth century.

Published by **About Comics**.
Publishing things that oughta be published.